P...og

C...der

Colin and Jacqui Hawkins

Collins

An imprint of HarperCollinsPublishers

First published in Great Britain by HarperCollins Publishers Ltd in 2001

1 3 5 7 9 10 8 6 4 2
ISBN: 0-00-710877-X

A CIP catalogue record for this title is available from the British Library.

The HarperCollins website address is: www.fireandwater.com

Printed and bound in Hong Kong

Captain and crew of the Mad Maggot 1740

DIRTY DAN

CAP'N BEN BLUNDER

BETTY BILGE

SWEATY SAM

CUTLASS KATE

NED SNUFF

ROVER

Captain's Log

Monday 10th June.

Snug as a weevil in bunk till noon. Then up
to find Dirty Dan had pinched all me
vittles. Parrot looking peaky, so we takes
him for a walk. Blow me if an 'orrid
big bird don't swoop down
and carry orf me hat!

Parrot squawkin', me hoppin' about
and yellin'. Dirty Dan laffin' like a drain.
Now I've got to buy a new hat.

Pirates are the scourge of the seven seas. Blink for a moment and these wicked and wily robbers will have the rings from your fingers and the bus pass from your purse. They will stop at nothing in their fierce quest for golden goodies and silver sparklies.

Hats

Should sit 'storm 'n' struggle snug'!

Cutlass

Shorter than sword so 'Cut less' 'Ha Har' (Pirate joke)

Three Quarters cutlass coat.

Spare cannon balls

Peg leg

Good leg.

Gob Yer Shut!

Telltale pirate signs
- Big hats
- Black patch
- Bright colours
- Gold buttons
- Peg Leg
- Parrot

"Knows't a pirate by the hook on his arm, the parrot, the black patch on his eye. Or, 'arken to the thud of his peg leg an' crutch as he crosses ye olde tavern."

There may be a pirate in your area.

Has anyone you know lost a parrot?

Know Yer Pirate

Captain's Log

4 of the clock.

We pops into 'Portholes and Peepers Emporium',
purveyors wot sells all manner of Piratical Paraphernalia.

I gets a new hat and Dirty Dan gets 'isself
a set of false teeth – very nice
they be and only two previous
owners. Dan says I look very
fetching in me new hat and
gives me a big kiss! Yuk!

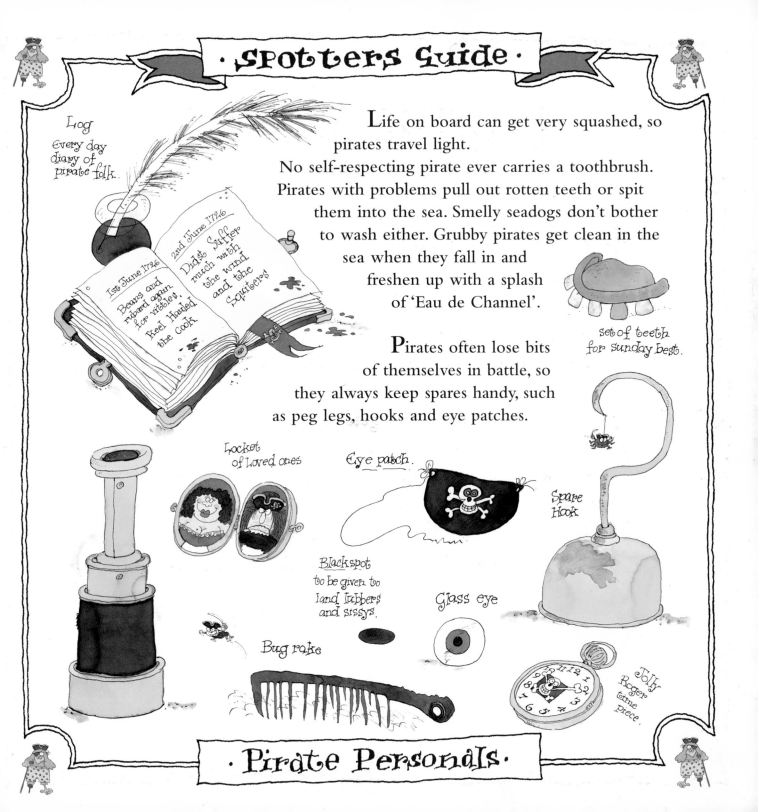

Life on board can get very squashed, so pirates travel light.
No self-respecting pirate ever carries a toothbrush. Pirates with problems pull out rotten teeth or spit them into the sea. Smelly seadogs don't bother to wash either. Grubby pirates get clean in the sea when they fall in and freshen up with a splash of 'Eau de Channel'.

Pirates often lose bits of themselves in battle, so they always keep spares handy, such as peg legs, hooks and eye patches.

Log
Every day diary of pirate folk.

1st June 1726
Beans and rhubarb again for vittles. Keel Hauled the Cook

2nd June 1726
Didst Suffer much with the wind and the Squitters

set of teeth for sunday best.

Locket of Loved ones

Eye patch.

Spare Hook

Blackspot to be given to land lubbers and sissys.

Glass eye

Bug rake

Jolly Roger time piece

· Pirate Personals ·

Captain's Log

6 of the clock

Me and Dan call in at the 'Mother Hubbard's Tea Rooms'. Share pot of tea for three, cucumber sandwiches and fairy cakes with 'ole Barty Roberts.

Barty do tell tall tales of far away places where they eat foreign grub like fried rice and oodles of noodles and prawn crackers.

He tells of a crew wot got kidnapped for their brass buttons in the China seas. No one believed Barty's tales and Dirty Dan said that he thought Barty was crackers.

Barty got the hump and went home early to read his Bible. I eats Barty's fairy cakes so as they wouldn't be wasted.

BARTHOLOMEW ROBERTS

A very strict pirate who made all his crew members be in their hammocks by eight o'clock. On Sundays he read the Bible to his crew, and never drank anything stronger than tea.

Get to sleep ye scurvey knaves tis gorn eight bells

Yes Sir

Aye Aye cap'n

OLAF THE VIKING

One of the earliest pirates. His gruesome giggling and loony laughter warned enemies of his approach.

Ha! Ha! Har! Ha!

CHIN YIN AND HIS KAI

Two notorious Chinese pirates who kidnapped a British crew and demanded a huge ransom. They thought the sailors' brass buttons were gold and that they must be very rich. They were wong.

Gosh Yes!

Will honerable gentleman give Yin and Kia lots of buttons?

Most Kind

Captain's Log

9 of the clock

At 'Big Bessie's Bar' for evening vittels of burnt black sausage and big chips and a bottle of fizzy grog, when, in bursts 'Blackie' Blackbeard. Blackie's beard is bigger and bushier than ever on account of Blackie sailin' the high seas fer months and months without 'aving packed shears nor razor. Dirty Dan said that he'd heard tell of an even bigger beard on an old pirate called Barbarossa who had never ever visited a Barber's shop in his life.

Blackie got a bit peeved and said that NO ONE EVER! EVER! EVER! HAD A BIGGER NOR BETTER BEARD THAN HIS! AND IT WOULD BE BETTER FOR DIRTY DAN IF HE THOUGHT SO TOO!!

Dan said Aye! Aye! Aye! That on further reflection no one could ever ever ever ever have a bigger or better beard than Blackie!

> Prithee Sir wouldst thou care to donate to the Eustace fund?

EUSTACE THE MONK

Also known as the 'Black Monk'. People said he had magic powers and could make his ship invisible. It was hard to cross the Channel without giving him a donation.

BARBAROSSA (REDBEARD)

This pest of a pirate plundered the coasts of France and Spain. Some people said that he dyed his beard with the blood of his enemies.

> mmm... tastes good.

> It's tomato ketchup really

> Avast! and Belay! or I'll cut ee' gizzerds orf!

BLACKBEARD (EDWARD TEACH)

One of the most fearsome looking pirates of all times. Blackbeard was extremely hairy, with an enormous black beard and hairy hands. His favourite trick was to go into battle with lighted tapers flaming in his beard.

Captain's Log

Tuesday 11th June - Sea calm.

Cast 'orf and catch the mornin' tide. Set sail for Barnacle Bay.
Ha! Har! Tis a grand life on the ocean waves!
Practise with new telescope. Everything looks black until
I take 'orf the lens cap...

Then arrghh!! See some
'orrible sights – especially
Sweaty Sam close up!!

Dirty Dan still grinning at everyone. Sea gets very
rough...up and down...up and down...up and
down...up and oorgh, not feeling so perky now...
...lost me old sea legs. Spend rest of day in bunk.

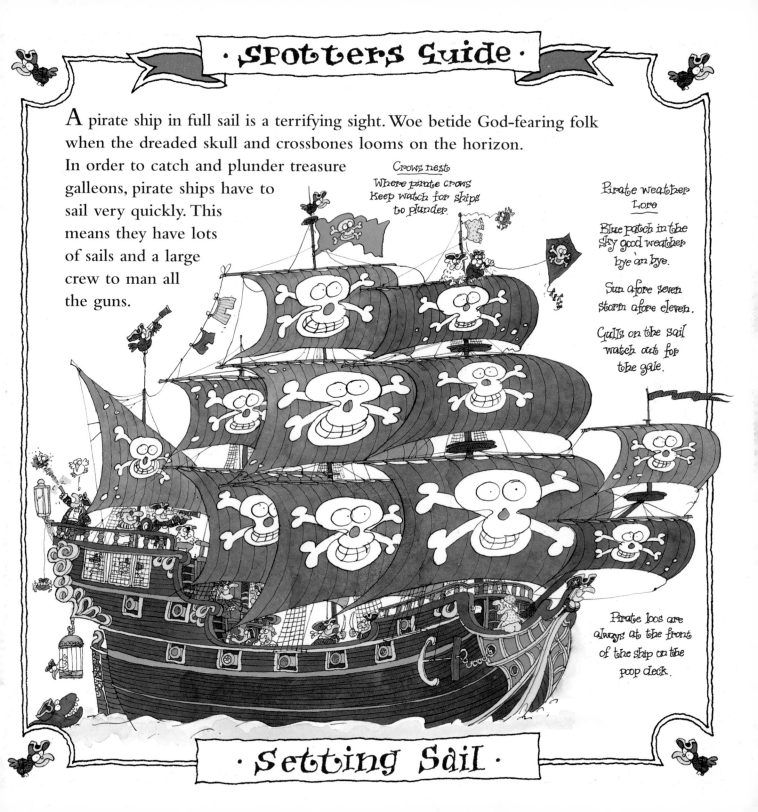

A pirate ship in full sail is a terrifying sight. Woe betide God-fearing folk when the dreaded skull and crossbones looms on the horizon.

In order to catch and plunder treasure galleons, pirate ships have to sail very quickly. This means they have lots of sails and a large crew to man all the guns.

Crows nest
Where pirate crows Keep watch for ships to plunder.

Pirate weather Lore

Blue patch in the sky good weather bye 'n bye.

Sun afore seven storm afore eleven.

Gulls on the sail watch out for the gale.

Pirate loos are always at the front of the ship on the poop deck.

· Setting Sail ·

Captain's Log

Wednesday 12th June.

Sea not so rough... Feeling a bit better.
Find me old sea legs – they was in me old sea
boots. Ha! Har! (Old pirate joke).

Sweaty Sam serves up lunch time vittles. Yuk! 'Tis 'orrid
smelly fish! Ooorgh! I do hate fish. Crew not sure either.
But Dan gets to try out his new teeth.
Betty Bilge has a go too. I eats some
tack - only a few maggots and
better than 'orrid fish!

Pirate grub is very boring, especially as everything goes rotten after a few days. But some pirate chefs do improvise with the odd seaweed souffle, grilled gull, or shark surprise.

Great sufferin' seaweed! Thar's maggots in me soup!

Sssh cap'n or they'll all be wanting them

A favourite treat is Figgie Dowdie. It's a sort of currant pudding.
"Figgie Dowdie is our favourite pud,
We get it when we're very good."

Mostly there's nothing to eat except hard biscuits called 'tack'. And they're usually full of horrible weavils and black spotted maggots. Some pirates love maggoty tack, others dunk the biscuits in their grog to improve the flavour. Hence the word 'tacky'.

Good Grief!

Open wide and pop inside

Old pirate rhyme:
"To eat hard tack
You need the knack
Or else yer pearlies
you will crack!"

Har! Har!

· Galleon Grub ·

Captain's Log

Thursday 13th June

Day break

Swear in old sea dog. Rover promises to be a loyal and true proper pirate pooch. Bless 'im.

Midday Sweaty Sam serves up more 'orrid fish. The crew are much peeved, they say that they is starting to look like fish. And that Sweaty Sam should walk the plank.

Sweaty says that if they lets him 'orf the plank he will make something really scrummy tomorrow. The crew say OK!

Mid-afternoon . Vote for Captain.

Usually nobody wants to be Cap'n so I gets the vote. But up pops Betty Bilge 'oo says that I ain't getting her vote! An' it's time fer a change! O' Lore!

Pirate crews always vote for their captains and captains have more fun. They get the biggest share of the booty, but they do have to give orders all the time and shout very loudly. This can be a big strain on their voices. Do you know anyone with a sore throat? Maybe your teacher has lost her voice?

Walking the plank is a popular method of disposing of an unwanted crew member. New pirates sign 'the pirate's charter' and swear on the Bible to be loyal and true crew members.

On long sea voyages pirates can pass the time playing games. You may know some of these: *Musical Hammocks, Hunt the Grog, Pass the Cannonball, Kiss Chase, Sharks (Pirate version of Sardines), What's the time Cap'n Hook?, Snarl (Pirate version of Snap).*

Captain's Log

Thursday 13th June.   Evening

Betty Bilge says it's time fer her to be Cap'n and Cutlass Kate agrees and says that the best pirates is women. Ned Snuff says that 'ee don't agree and 'ee don't want any girlie Cap'n cos girls are sissy.

Betty changes Ned's opinion about girls with a smack round the chops with a wet fish!

Everyone much impressed by Betty's persuasive argument and all agree that she can be Cap'n till we gets back to Barnacle Bay.

Even mums can be pirates. Do you know of a mum with a frightening gaze and a heartening cry – "Tidy your bunk! Ha, Har! Scrub yer teeth!" Does this sound like your mum? Does your mum dish up hard tack for tea?

Anne Bonney and Mary Read were notorious lady pirates of days gone by. This fearsome pair struck terror in the hearts of friends and foe alike. Especially if a pirate was not polite and forgot to say "please" and "thank you".

Captain's Log

Friday 14th June · Morning

Cap'n Betty says that all the crew do niff 'orrid and fowl. And
that all the crew's clobber is to be washed. Much moaning by crew
but Betty waves her wet fish and says she's Cap'n
and she ain't sufferin' no more stinky-phoo crew!

11 of the clock.

Crew all washing their togs starkers
when the crow's nest shouts, "Sail on the
starboard bow!"

O'Lore! 'Tis Commander Roger Jolly in the HMS Hornet.
What a clamity with everyone's clobber in the wash...
We is doomed! "Stop yer fretin' yer lily-livered weasles, I have a plan-"
yells Betty B. "Yer can all wear me spare dresses and pretend to be
landed ladies out on a sea cruise."

continued ..

Pirates love to play tricks. One favourite pirate prank is to fly the flag of honest sea-faring folk and sneak up on an unsuspecting treasure ship. At the last moment, the wily weasels hoist the Jolly Roger and leap on board.

Another pirate trick is to pretend to be ladies in distress. Gallant sailors who hasten to rescue these damsels of the seas are rewarded with the sharp point of a cutlass in the gut. The sight of a great, hairy pirate in a bonnet and petticoat will haunt many an old sea salt to the end of his days.

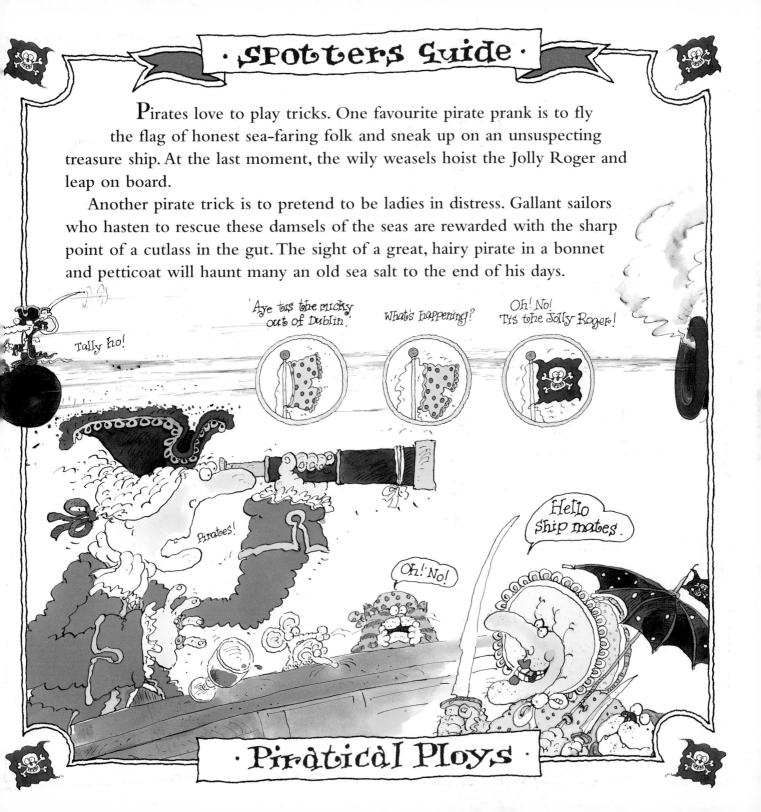

Tally ho!

'Aye tis the micky out of Dublin.'

What's happening?

Oh! No! Tis the Jolly Roger!

Pirates!

Oh! No!

Hello ship mates.

· Piratical Ploys ·

Captain's Log

Friday 14th June.

Well snogle me wurts, Betty B's rum plan worked a treat. Commander Jolly was so 'orrified when he spies such a giggling gaggle of hairy ladies, all blowin' kisses at 'im, that he do put up every yard of sail and do breeze off fast as the wind can take 'im. Ha! Har! Ha! Har!

We was so delighted to escape the clutches of Commander Jolly that we decides to 'ave a party. Much fiddlin' and singin' of shanties, munchin' maggoty biscuits and guzzlin' fizzy grog.

Then Sweaty Sam serves up 'is surprise grub. "Tuck in shipmates!" says Sam, "it be Ssshark Sssshurprise!" Everyone is really surprised, especially the shark!

It is vital for a pirate ship to have a band on board. Singing and dancing are an important part of pirate therapy.

As evening draws in, weary pirates blink blearily into the flickering lamplight, and hanging in hammocks, hum happily as the accordionist plays. Many a sea shanty can be heard wafting over the moonlit waves on a still night.

Another function of the band is to play loudly as the pirates go into battle. The awful banging of the drums, the piercing screech of the violins and the yowling of the crew, strike terror into the hearts of the enemy.

Captain's Log

Evening. 10 of the clock.

Weather fair, sea calm. Tucked up in hammock with flaggon of hot chocolate. Good night ship mates, sleep tight. Don't let the bugs bite! Ha! Ha!